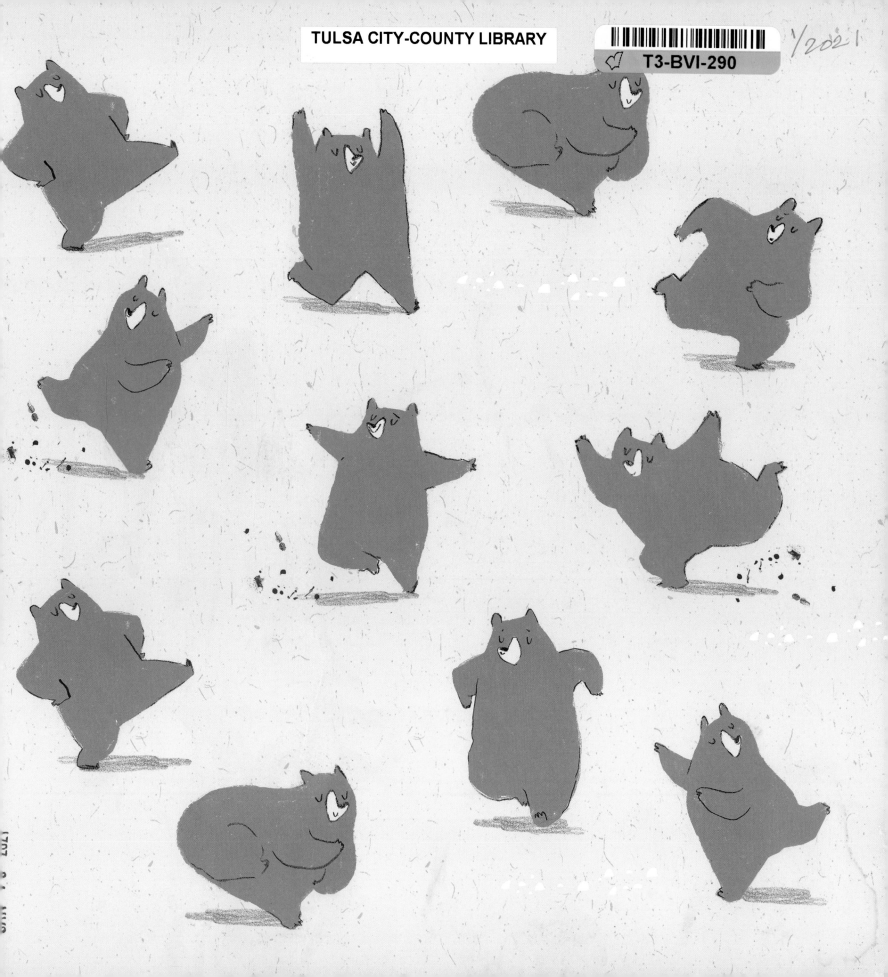

THE BIG TRIP

Alex Willmore

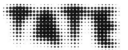

This is Bear.

Bear likes to strut his stuff.

Bear had all the best moves and he thought that he looked so . . .

so . . .

cool.

He was probably the coolest in the whole forest.

Bear never looked where he
was going, but Bear didn't care.

He was far too cool and important.

It didn't matter who was in Bear's way.

He **barged** past fox . . .

and sent snake **flying** through the air!

Stepped on tortoise . . .

Because Bear liked to strut his stuff **everywhere**

and he didn't care
who was in his way!

One day, Bear was out strutting his stuff as normal when he came across Moose.

"Woah there!"
said Moose.

"You should really look
where you're going!"

"I do what I want!"
huffed Bear.

Moose was very
much in the way,
but Bear didn't care

Bear **pushed** and shoved . . .

and **heaved** and hoed . . .

But Moose
just
wouldn't
budge!

"Hey Bear, you can't just go around doing whatever you want, pushing everyone around." said Moose.

"The forest is for everyone and you need to take care!"

Bear didn't think that sounded fun at all. He stepped around Moose, poked out his tongue . . .

and took a step backwards . . .

Bear tripped . . .

wobbled . . .

stumbled . . .

bounced . . .

and fell down a big hill!

He CRASHED into a bird's nest – **BOOF!**

SMASHED through a bee hive –

BZZZZZZ

. . . and eventually came to a stop in a smelly swamp at the bottom of a deep dark hole.

Bear didn't feel so cool anymore.
In fact, he felt very silly and all alone.

He sniffed. He could hear all the
other animals laughing at him.

"Serves him right!" said Frog.

"Hahaha!" laughed Fox, pointing.

"Hey now guys," said Moose.
"None of us are perfect, right? We
all make mistakes from time to time.
What do you say we help him out?"

They looked at each other.
"I suppose . . ."

As Bear sat all alone in the dark he wished that
he had looked where he was going, and that he'd
thought about more than just himself.

"I suppose I've been a very careless bear." He sighed.

But just then, out of the darkness came a hand.

Fox, Frog, Snake, Moose and all the
other animals heaved and hoed
and pulled Bear out of the swamp.

Bear was embarassed, a little bit
soggy and very, very grateful.

He smiled shyly, "Thanks everyone."
he said softly.

The very next day, Bear set about putting things right.

"Comfy?"

"There we go!"

Now when Bear goes out to strut his stuff, he isn't alone anymore and he always looks where he's going!

Well. Most of the time.

For Mum - A.W.

First published 2020 by order of the Tate Trustees
by Tate Publishing, a division of Tate Enterprises Ltd,
Millbank, London SW1P 4RG
www.tate.org.uk/publishing

Text and illustrations © Alex Willmore 2020

A catalogue record for this book is available from the British Library

ISBN 978 1 84976 690 6

Distributed in the United States and Canada by ABRAMS, New York
Library of Congress Control Number applied for

Colour reproduction by Evergreen Colour Management Ltd
Printed and bound in China by C&C Offset Printing Co., Ltd

FSC
www.fsc.org

MIX
Paper from
responsible sources
FSC® C008047